The first book:
Tess's story

The second book:
Mike's story

The third book:
Lizzie's story

The Travellers: Ben
by Rosemary Hayes

Published by Ransom Publishing Ltd.
Unit 7, Brocklands Farm, West Meon, Hampshire GU32 1JN, UK
www.ransom.co.uk

ISBN   978 178127 970 0
First published in 2015

Ben

The fourth book in the series

Rosemary Hayes

Ransom

Acknowledgements

My thanks to everyone who has made time to tell me about the lives of Gypsy/Romany/Travellers, how they live now and how they lived in the past, particularly to those in Cambridgeshire County Council who work with the GRT community and to Gordon Boswell of The Romany Museum, Spalding, Lincolnshire.

I am very grateful to the following members of GRT families who have welcomed me into their homes and talked to me about their experiences:

Brady
Linda
Andrew
Rene
Jessie
Abraham
Abi
and Rita.

The English gypsies I spoke to referred to themselves as either gypsies or travellers, and these terms appear to be interchangeable. Many have Romany roots and still practise some of the old traditions and use words from the Romany language.

Traveller Organisations

The Community Law Partnership (CLP) incorporates the Travellers' Advice Team, a nationwide 24-hour advice service for gypsies and travellers.

The National Federation of Gypsy Liaison Groups

The Gypsy Council

Friends, Families and Travellers

National Association of Gypsy and Traveller Officers

Travellers' Times

The story so far ...

Ben lives with his mum, Kate, and his younger sister, Tess. Ben is 16 and wants to be a professional footballer.

At school Ben and his friends are always taunting Mike, a gypsy boy in their class, and Ben hates the fact that Tess is friendly with Mike and that she rides the gypsy horses.

One day, Ben discovers that Mike has taken Tess to a horse fair; he is furious and attacks Mike. They have a serious fight, but Ben comes off worse.

Both boys are sent to the head teacher and Ben is

forced to apologise to Mike for bad-mouthing the gypsies. This makes him determined not to go back to school next term.

One

Every day now, Ben dreaded seeing his mum. She was really stressing him out. He tried to avoid her, but today she had come home from work early. He tried to creep up the stairs to his room, but she heard him.

'Not so fast, Ben,' shouted Kate. 'We need to talk.'

Ben walked slowly back down the stairs. Kate was waiting for him.

'Come and sit down,' she said.

Ben followed her into the lounge, but he didn't sit down. He stood facing her, his arms folded.

'I know what you're going to say, Mum. But I've *told* you. I'm not going back to school next term. I want to be a footballer.'

Kate sighed. 'Listen, love, you have to be a really good footballer if you want to make a career of it.'

'I *am* good. And I'm going for a trial next week for the under-eighteens. You know that.'

Kate turned away and looked out of the window. 'But what if you don't get selected?'

'Then I'll find a job,' he said.

'What sort of job can you get? Your GCSE predictions are dire. You'll probably have to do retakes.'

'Retakes. No way! I've finished with school.'

'Ben, if you worked harder … '

'Just because I'm not a boff like Tess!'

'Don't be like that … '

Ben didn't answer. He left the room, slamming the door behind him.

He went out of the house and walked down to the recreation ground, kicking angrily at any loose pebbles. When he got to the rec he sat on the swings, idly pushing himself backwards and forwards.

Then he had to move because some woman with a load of small kids came along.

He mooched around the edge of the field, frowning. So far the holidays had been horrible. None of his mates were around and his mum kept giving him grief.

He stopped and leant on the fence, looking into the distance. There was nothing for him here in this deadbeat place. Football was his way out of here. He *had* to do well in the trials.

He'd been leaning on the fence for a while when he noticed the car. A shiny, brand new model circling slowly round the rec. Ben watched it.

A Merc! What I'd do to drive that!

The man driving it saw him looking. He stopped the car and got out. He was wearing an expensive-looking jacket and his dark black sunglasses hid his eyes.

He started walking towards Ben and, as he got closer, he waved.

'Hi there. It's Ben, isn't it?'

Ben frowned. 'Yeah,' he said. He couldn't place the guy. How did he know his name? He couldn't believe anyone who drove a car like that would know him. Unless he was a football scout or something. Ben's heart began to race. Maybe he'd been spotted! But the next moment, his hopes were dashed.

'You're the brother of that lass who's friendly with the gypsies, aren't you?'

Ben was embarrassed. 'Yeah,' he mumbled. 'She likes their horses.'

'Your family's got some reputation round here,' said the man.

'What d'you mean?'

The man took off his sunglasses. He looked around, but there was no one who could hear them.

'Young Tess, she shouldn't be getting in with the likes of them,' said the man. 'They're all sorts of trouble.'

Ben bit his lip. 'You can't tell her,' he said. 'She won't listen.'

'Well, let's hope she knows what she's doing.'

The man came nearer and stuck out his hand. 'My name's Jim Blackwood.'

Ben shook his hand and they leant over the fence together.

'So what are you up to, Ben? Still at school?'

Ben shook his head.

'Looking for a job?'

'I want to be a footballer.'

Why was he telling this guy?

The man clicked his tongue. 'Hey, that's a tough call.'

'I know. But I'm going for a trial next week.'

'Well, I'm impressed. Good luck, son. And if it doesn't work out, come and see me; I might be able to find you a job.'

'What sort of job?'

Blackwood nodded over towards his car. 'D'you like cars?'

'Sure'

He rubbed his nose. 'Well, I might find you something … you come and see me when you're ready.'

'Where do you live?'

Blackwood looked away. 'I usually come down to the rec most days,' he said. 'You can always find me here.'

'Thanks,' said Ben. 'I'll do that … if the football doesn't work out.'

Blackwood turned and walked away. As he got into his car, he raised his hand, then he gunned the engine and the car moved off, making an expensive purring sound.

When Ben got home, he didn't say anything to Kate about his talk with Blackwood, but she noticed he was in a better mood. He even put the rubbish out for her.

'Thanks, love,' she said. 'You seem a bit happier.'

Ben smiled. 'Yeah,' he said.

'Dad just rang,' said Kate. 'He wants to go to the trial with you.'

'What … he's coming here?'

Mum looked away. 'Yes.'

'Great,' said Ben.

Ben's dad didn't visit much. He lived a long way away, with his new wife and baby.

I'll have to do well if Dad's coming.

It had always been Dad's dream for Ben to get taken on to train for the squad, and he was *so* close. Dad would be over the moon if he made it.

Tess came in a bit later. Ben screwed up his nose. 'Phew, you stink of horse,' he said.

She ignored him and headed for the stairs.

'Still, I suppose the riding stable's better than that gypsy site,' he muttered.

Tess stopped, her foot on the first stair. 'Oh shut it, Ben. There's nothing wrong with the site, or the people who live there.'

'Filthy gypsies,' muttered Ben.

'Filthy! You should see their vans and the day rooms. They're spotless. A lot cleaner than your disgusting room.'

'You want to be careful, Tess,' said Ben.

'What do you mean?'

'There's gossip about you in the village.'

Tess turned round and faced him. 'What sort of gossip?'

'People are saying you shouldn't get involved with their sort.'

'What people?'

Ben wasn't going to tell her about Blackwood. He shrugged. 'I hear stuff.'

'Oh for goodness sake, Ben,' yelled Tess, stamping her foot. 'I thought you'd stopped all that rubbish.'

Kate came out of the kitchen. 'What's all this shouting?'

'Ben's being horrible about the gypsy families.'

'I'm only warning her, Mum. People are talking. She shouldn't get so friendly with them.'

'Ben, I don't know how you can say that,' said Kate. 'You've never been to the site, you've never met any of the families.'

'What d'you mean? I was at school with Mike and his mates. They were big trouble.'

'And you weren't?' Kate was looking angry. 'What about that time when you picked a fight with Mike?'

'He started it!'

'That's not what I heard.'

They faced off against each other, neither willing to back down.

Then Kate turned to Tess. 'Dad's coming here next week.'

'Great. Can I show him Flame?'

'Not that damn gypsy horse again,' muttered Ben, but neither Kate nor Tess took any notice.

Kate hesitated. 'You'd have to ask him. He's coming on Wednesday morning and he'll be at the football trials in the afternoon. Perhaps he could go to the riding stables afterwards.'

'Why don't you come too, Mum?' asked Tess.

Kate smiled. 'I've seen plenty of Flame.'

'I mean come with Dad.'

But Kate shook her head.

Ben hardly slept the night before the trials. He was up early, his kit all ready, and he was sitting in the kitchen, his hands round a mug of tea, when Kate came down.

'Hey, you're early!'

'Didn't sleep much,' he muttered.

Kate came and put her arms round his shoulders. 'Try and relax, love.'

But Ben's foot was tapping the floor and he looked pale.

Kate brought him some toast and sat down beside him. 'I know it means a lot, this trial,' she said, 'but it's not the end of the world if you don't make the squad.'

'It is to me,' muttered Ben. He pushed the toast away.

'You should eat something.'

'Don't feel like it.'

Tess came in, rubbing her eyes. She helped herself to some breakfast and then went upstairs again. Moments later she was down, dressed in her riding things and heading for the door.

'Good luck, Ben,' she shouted, waving at him as she biked off.

Mum left for work not long after this and Ben was alone. Dad wouldn't be here for another hour. Ben couldn't settle to anything. He tried playing a game on his computer, but he couldn't concentrate. He tried watching some of the footie games he'd recorded, but these made him feel even more nervous. When Dad finally rang the door bell, he was pacing up and down the passage, his sports bag all ready.

'How you feeling, son?' asked Dad, grinning broadly as he pushed past Ben and headed for the kitchen. 'Tess not here?'

Ben shook his head. 'Gone to the stables. And you can relax, Mum's gone to work.'

Dad didn't say anything, but Ben noticed that the tension drained from his face.

'We've got ages yet,' he said. 'Let's have a cuppa and a chat.'

'No, Dad. Can we go, please? I really want to get there. There might be bad traffic or something … '

Dad raised his eyebrows. 'It's not far, Ben, but if it makes you happy, OK, let's go.'

Two

It wasn't far and there wasn't that much traffic. Dad was right. They were really early and they sat outside the stadium waiting for the others.

'Cambridge United,' said Dad. 'How many matches have we been to, Ben?'

'Dunno. Masses.'

That had been in the good times, when Dad was around and they'd go every Saturday, whether the 'U's were playing at home or away. Dad had followed the team since he was a boy.

'It's good to be back,' he said. 'And I never thought a son of mine would be trying out for the junior squad. I was never as good as you, Ben.'

Ben was feeling sick 'I might not make it, Dad,' he said.

'Even if you don't, you've got further than I ever did.' Dad noticed Ben's pale face and clenched fists. He put his hand on Ben's knee.

'Relax, it's not the end of the world if ... '

'Don't. That's what Mum keeps saying.'

Dad didn't answer.

At last the others arrived: the current junior squad, the coach, a few of the proper team, a few hopeful youngsters like him and some other men Ben didn't recognize. Ben knew some of the other boys trying out for the squad; two of them were school friends and they looked as nervous as he felt.

The adult players were all big and strong, and Ben felt weedy beside them, but they were all friendly and made Ben and the other boys feel welcome. These were blokes that Ben had watched every Saturday. He was in awe of them.

All the boys sat on the bench at the side of the ground while the coach spoke to them.

'We'll do some warm-up exercises together,' he

said. 'Then we'll mix you all up into the two teams and see how you get on.'

He asked what positions the boys usually played. Ben had always been a striker in the school team, but two of the other lads said they were strikers, too. They were bigger and stronger than Ben.

'OK,' said the coach. 'We'll give you turns, change you round a bit.' He pointed to the other two lads. 'You two start as strikers,' he said, then he turned to Ben. 'And you can be a midfielder.'

Ben had hardly ever played in midfield, but he didn't dare argue.

The coach noticed Ben's reaction.

'Don't worry,' he said, patting him on the back. 'We'll change you over.'

Ben bit his lip. He saw his dad nearby, sitting in the empty stands, his hands on his knees, frowning. When Ben caught his eye, Dad smiled at him and gave him a thumbs up.

Ben had never played at this level before. He'd known the adult players would be much better, of course they were, they were professional, but the junior squad was brilliant, too. And the ball never seemed to come Ben's way. Or, if it did, he wasn't fast enough to get to it before his opponent.

And the marking! In school games, he could usually outrun his marker, but here his marker stuck to him all the time. He could never shake him off, and when the other guy got possession of the ball, Ben couldn't keep up.

After fifteen minutes the coach blew his whistle and the game stopped.

Ben bent over, his hands on his knees, taking deep breaths.

Maybe now I'll get a chance to be a striker.

But the coach put him even further down the field.

'Ben, you try left full back,' he said.

What? I'm never going to be able to show him what I can do.

Ben got into position and for the next fifteen minutes he hardly saw the ball. All the action was at the other end of the pitch.

Later, there were more changes.

At least my legs are still fresh.

'Right, Ben. You're second striker now.'

At last! Now I can show him.

The whistle went again for the game to resume. Ben was playing for the other side now and one of the professionals – one of Ben's heroes – was the main striker. He smiled as Ben went to take up his position.

'We'll show them, eh Ben?'

Ben blushed and nodded.

I must do well.

But he tried too hard, rushed all over the place, panicking. Time and again one of the professionals or one of the juniors would set him up, pass the ball to him and he'd fail to get onto it.

And then, suddenly, it was all over.

The coach thanked them all for coming and the juniors and professionals went back into the changing rooms. Ben and the other boys stayed behind.

'Lots of potential among you lads,' said the coach, rubbing his hands. 'Spoilt for choice.' Then he went on to explain some technical points, where they should have been at different stages of the game, formations and such like.

'All right, boys,' said the coach at last. 'Off you go now. I'll let you know if any of you are selected for the squad.' He hesitated. 'As you know, we can only take three next season, so don't be too disappointed if you haven't made it this time. You can try again next year.'

Next year. There won't be a next year. If I don't get in this time I'll have to get a job.

In the car going back, Ben was quiet.

'Well done, son,' said Dad. 'You gave it your best shot.'

Ben balled his fist. 'No I didn't, I messed up,' he muttered.

'Well,' said Dad carefully. 'It was hard for you, being put in midfield first and then as a defender. You're not used to those positions.'

'The coach knew what he was doing,' said Ben. 'I'd never have gone the distance as a striker.'

'Umm,' said Dad. 'They were very fast, those juniors.'

'I'm not good enough, Dad. I'll never be that fast.'

'The coach said you had potential, Ben. Let's just wait and see what happens. You never know. He might still want you. And, if not, there's always next year; you've still got some growing to do. You'll be bigger and stronger then. You can stay on at school and try again next year.

'Not you too! I don't want to go back to school, Dad. It's a waste of time. I want to be in the squad NOW!'

His dad didn't answer.

When they got back to the house, Mum was home from work. There wasn't much going on at the Tech during the summer, but there were conferences and other stuff, so she still had to be there part-time at least.

Mum ignored Dad then turned to Ben.

'How did it go, love?'

'Not so good,' he said. Then suddenly, looking at Mum's face, he wanted to cry. He wanted to throw himself down and blub like a baby.

He'd never be a professional footballer. Who the hell was he kidding?

'Well,' said Mum. 'We'll wait and see, shall we?' Then she turned to Dad.

'I hope you'll have time to go to the riding stables. Tess is waiting for you there.'

'Yeah! Tess,' shouted Ben. 'It's all about my kid sister, isn't it! Tess is the star of this family, isn't she? The clever one, the brilliant rider. The gypsy-lover!'

Dad looked up sharply. 'What do you mean ... ?'

'Ask Mum,' yelled Ben.

Kate reached out to him but he ducked under her arm, dropped his sports bag in the hall, ran up the stairs to his room and flung himself on his bed.

Ben couldn't fight back the tears any longer. He sobbed, pounding his fist into his pillow. When at last he stopped crying, he sniffed and sat up.

He'd get a job then, earn some money, move out of home. He'd show them.

Downstairs, Mum and Dad were shouting at each other and Ben heard the words 'Tess' and 'gypsies' floating up the stairs.

Three

A few days later, the coach rang Ben.

'Sorry, Ben. Try again next year; you've got a lot of potential. '

Although Ben had been expecting it, he still felt really disappointed. Dad rang and he had to break the news to him.

'I didn't make it, Dad.'

'Never mind, Ben. You'll be bigger and stronger next year.'

'Yeah. You said that before.'

Some of his mates had come home and Ben hung out with them for a while, but he got fed up with hearing about their brilliant holidays.

'You been away, Ben?'

'No.'

'Oh yeah, you were trying for the footie squad. How did it go?'

'I didn't make it.'

'Bad luck, mate.'

He was sick of everyone feeling sorry for him. Mum, Dad, his friends – even Tess was being nicer to him than usual.

'Sorry about the squad, Ben,' she'd said.

'As if you care,' muttered Ben.

He went out of the house. He didn't want her sympathy. He didn't want anyone's sympathy.

He went to the rec again and sat down on a bench. His phone vibrated and he saw that there was a text from one of his mates.

We're meeting up in town. Can u come?

What's the point. I haven't got any money and I can't stand hearing any more talk about what they did on holiday.

He played with his phone for a while. More texts and more holiday photos on Facebook.

Everyone else seemed to be having a great time,

have plans. Everyone except him. He switched off the phone and stared into space.

He'd messed up. He'd not bothered to work at school and now he'd not been taken on by the squad, either. He stood up and stuck his hands in his pockets, kicking at the grass.

He wondered whether the Blackwood guy would turn up again.

Bet he didn't mean it when he said he could give me a job.

He wandered round the village, but there was nothing to do here. He heard a train in the distance and looked towards the railway line.

Wish I could take the train and never come back.

He was so deep in his own thoughts that at first he didn't hear the car draw up ahead of him and stop.

It was the Blackwood guy again. He wound down the car window and shouted to Ben. Ben looked up and Blackwood turned off the engine, got out of the car and came towards him.

'You OK, Ben?'

Ben shrugged. 'S'pose so.'

'You didn't make the squad then?'

Ben shook his head.

'You thought any more about doing some work for me?'

Ben frowned. 'Do you mean it?'

'Sure. I could use a bright lad like you.'

Bright lad. As if.

'What sort of work?'

Blackwood smiled, but he didn't meet Ben's eyes. 'Come and sit in the car,' he said, glancing round to see if anyone else was about. 'I'll tell you.'

Ben sat in the front seat, sinking down into the plush leather. He'd never been in such an expensive car.

'Like it?' asked Blackwood.

Ben nodded. 'It's brilliant.'

'Well, if you do some jobs for me, maybe you'll get to drive it sometimes.'

Ben's head jerked up. 'D'you mean it?' Then, immediately, 'But I'm not seventeen yet. I couldn't get a licence.'

'Oh, we'll sort something out,' said Blackwood, smoothly.

He leant over and took something out of the glove compartment. 'Here,' he said. 'Have a spliff.'

Ben hesitated. He'd smoked before; he and his mates had often shared a fag round the back of the sports hall at school, but he'd never had a spliff.

Blackwood watched him as he took his first puff.

Soon Ben started to feel more relaxed. Blackwood told him about the jobs.

'Just delivering stuff for me,' he said. 'And collecting money for the goods.'

'And you'll pay me?'

Blackwood smiled. 'Of course I'll pay you, Ben. When you collect the money, you'll have your cut.'

Ben frowned and Blackwood went on. 'It's regular work, son. I got a lot of customers round here. I can't be delivering all the stuff, so I need some helpers.'

'So, I collect the ... '

'Yeah, you collect the packages from me. I tell you where to go to deliver them.'

'What? They're all round here then, your customers?'

Blackwood's eyes slid away from Ben's. 'Not all of them. You can start with the local ones. See how you go.'

Ben didn't answer.

'And,' continued Blackwood, 'I'll let you use my little car at first, then when you're a bit more experienced you can have a go with this one.'

'I haven't had driving lessons.'

Blackwood burst out laughing. 'I can teach you all you want to know.' He put his hand on Ben's knee. 'How about it? You want to earn some money, don't you?'

'Yeah. Sure.'

'Good lad. You can start tonight. Meet me back here at seven o'clock and I'll hand over some goods and tell you where to go.'

Blackwood turned the key in the ignition and Ben started to get out of the car.

'And no need to tell anyone you're working for me, Ben. That'll be our little secret. OK?'

Ben frowned. Why was he not surprised. 'Sure,' he said.

He closed the passenger door – it shut with a soft clunk – and stood in the road as Blackwood drove off.

The effect of the spliff hadn't worn off and he felt good as he made his way home. He started laughing.

His secret. A secret from his family and friends.

It was easy. Every evening he met up with Blackwood in a different place, then he'd be given the packages to deliver. The addresses were all local, all easy to get to, either on foot or by bus. He just had to deliver them and collect the money.

Back home, though, Mum continued to nag him.

'You've got to think of the future, Ben,' she kept saying.

'Give me a break, will you?' he replied. 'Can't you just wait until the exam results are out, at least?'

He knew they'd be bad, but it bought him some time.

Mum had raised her eyebrows. 'You said yourself you'd done badly, Ben. And your teachers …'

'All right, all right, leave me alone.'

'I'm only thinking of you, Ben. You can't hang around doing nothing. If you refuse to go back to school, then you'll have to get out there and earn some money.'

If only she knew! He fingered the notes in his pocket.

Her next remark brought him up short. 'And where are you going in the evenings, Ben? What are you doing?'

'I told you. Just hanging out with friends.'

She frowned. 'You've changed, Ben,' she said slowly. 'It's as if you don't care about anything.'

He shrugged and went out.

He hated the atmosphere at home. He couldn't tell Kate what he was doing, but she was obviously suspicious. Perhaps if he earned enough, he could move out.

He'd never asked Blackwood what was in the packages he delivered, but he knew – and he kept smoking the spliffs to block out what he was doing.

Sometimes he was surprised by the people who bought the goods. He wasn't surprised that other teenagers were using, but some of the other kids were really young.

Supposing it had been his kid sister, Tess? But he killed the thought as soon as it popped into his head.

Ben kept all the information to himself. He would never let on about *them*, and *they* would never say who delivered their stuff.

'Just as long as you keep your mouth shut, Ben,' Blackwood said. 'Then everyone's happy.'

Ben knew that if he ever grassed on them, Blackwood would hear of it and he'd be in big trouble. Blackwood had told him that he had 'backers', whatever that meant.

I'll get something else soon. Another job.

But Blackwood wouldn't like that, would he?

Blackwood was as good as his word, and one day he took Ben to some land he said he owned. It was a long way off the road, with no neighbours to see what was going on, and he let Ben drive the little car. It was a bit bashed up, with a dent in the boot, but there was nothing else wrong with it, and before long Ben was driving down the lanes, reversing, doing wheelies, bombing around with confidence. He loved it.

'You're a natural, Ben,' said Blackwood. 'Now you can drive, you can do more work for me, go to other places.'

'But ... '

Blackwood put an arm round Ben's shoulders. 'Don't worry about a licence, son. You won't get caught, will you?'

Four

Ben knew there'd be a showdown at home. He'd been working for Blackwood for three weeks now, and he'd been out every evening and sleeping late in the mornings.

'Sit down Ben,' said Kate, one day. 'We need to have a serious talk.'

'Not again,' muttered Ben.

Kate folded her arms. 'What are you doing every evening?'

'I *told* you … '

'Don't lie to me, Ben. None of your friends have seen you recently.'

'What! How do you know?'

'I talk to their parents.'

'What!! You've been checking up on me. How dare you!'

'If you were being honest with me I wouldn't have to, would I? Now, I want to know what you are doing.'

Ben looked down at the ground. What could he say? He'd promised Blackwood he'd keep quiet.

'I've been learning about cars,' he said, at last.

Kate frowned. 'What do you mean?'

'I've been working for a guy who has ... has a garage. He's been teaching me about engines and that.'

It sounded unlikely. Even he realised that.

'This guy, what's his name?'

Ben hesitated. 'He's called John Davis.'

'Where did you meet him?'

Ben shifted his legs. 'Oh, he's a friend of a mate. You won't know him. He lives way out in the fens.'

'But why can't you work for him during the day? Why do you work in the evenings?'

Ben swallowed. He was getting in too deep.

'He's trying to build up a business,' he said. 'But he has to work somewhere else during the day.'

How easily the lies came.

Kate frowned. 'But is this leading anywhere, Ben? Is he paying you?'

'Yeah. A bit.'

More than a bit.

Ben went on, almost believing the lie. 'Then, when he sets up on his own, he'll give me a proper job.'

'I see,' said Kate, but she was still frowning.

Just before he went out that evening, he heard Kate talking to his dad on the phone.

'Yes, he seems happier. Apparently he's doing a bit of work for some mechanic.'

Ben smiled to himself. Mechanic! As if.

He let himself out of the door as quietly as he could. He didn't want Kate to question him again. He'd got into a routine, now. He'd meet Blackwood at the rec or somewhere else in the village, be given the packages and the addresses, then walk to where he'd parked the little car, plug in the sat nav and drive off to make the deliveries.

At first he'd been really scared at driving without a licence, keeping an eye out, all the time, for police, and driving very carefully. But he was more relaxed now. It was easy.

He'd go all over the place. Never to people's homes, but usually to a meeting place by a public building or in a park.

The handovers were done quickly, the people he met ready with the cash and anxious to get going as soon as possible. Sometimes they hardly spoke.

That suited Ben fine.

The next day he'd hand over the cash and Blackwood would count it and give him his cut.

Nothing to it! Easy money.

Then one evening, as he looked at the address on one of the packages, his heart started to race.

It was the address of the gypsy site. But Blackwood had called them 'filthy gypsies'. What was he doing, dealing with the likes of them?

He made the other deliveries first, then drove nervously down to the site. The instructions were to meet the client in a lane just before the entrance.

It was getting dark as he drove past the Tech, under the motorway bridge and up the potholed road towards the site. He'd never been there before and he felt a stab of fear in his gut. He saw the lane, slowed up and killed the engine.

There was no one there. No one waiting for him.

He felt uneasy. This had never happened before.

He waited for ten minutes, then he phoned Blackwood, but the phone went to voicemail. Blackwood had told him never to leave a message.

Ben sat in the gathering dark, biting his lip. He was just about to turn the car round and drive away when he saw a figure walking down the lane towards him.

At last.

Quickly, he got out of the car, the package in his hand, and walked towards the figure. As he got nearer, the other person spoke.

'Ben?'

He froze. He recognized that voice. He doubled back towards the car, but the other person was too quick, running to head him off. They both reached the car together.

'What the hell are you doing down here?'

'Mike?' Ben's voice was hoarse.

'Who's that for?' said Mike, pointing at the package that Ben was trying to hide behind his back.

'No one. It's a mistake … sorry. I'd better go.'

But Mike lunged forward and grabbed Ben's arm. He twisted it until the package fell to the ground.

'Let go of me, will you!'

Mike took no notice. Still holding onto Ben's arm, he bent down and picked up the package, weighing it in his hand.

'Who's it for, Ben?' he repeated.

'I tell you. I don't know,' hissed Ben. 'I was just told to meet someone down here. Believe me, I didn't want to come.'

'Didn't want to visit the dirty gypsies, eh?'

'I didn't say that.'

'No, but that's what you meant, isn't it?'

Ben tried to wriggle free, but Mike's grip was too strong. He didn't want to get into another fight – and Mike had back-up – all his friends and family at the site.

Ben was really scared now. 'Sorry, Mike, I didn't mean to … ' he stuttered.

'Didn't mean to *what*? Insult me and my family?'

'Yeah.'

Mike released his arm. 'You've given us nothing but grief, Ben. At school, in the village.'

'Sorry.'

'Huh! You *say* sorry but you don't mean it, do

you? You'll be back to bad-mouthing us as soon as you're home in your safe little house.'

Ben didn't answer.

'Pity you're not more like your sister. She's got more guts than you'll ever have. She's stood up for us right from the start.'

Ben didn't answer.

'You'd better go now,' said Mike. 'And take your drugs with you. I don't know who's using here and I don't want to know.'

Ben scrambled away towards the car and Mike watched him, his hands in his pockets. Then he frowned into the darkness and walked round to the back of the car noticing the dent in the boot.

'Hey, I've seen that car before.

Ben made to open the driver's door, but Mike barred his way.

'I know who owns this car. It's that bastard who got me and Johnny into trouble.'

'What?'

Suddenly, Mike grabbed Ben's shoulders. 'What's he call himself now?'

Mike was shaking him hard and Ben was really scared. 'Get off me. He's ... called Blackwood.'

Still Mike didn't let him go. 'Huh! Blackwood is

it? That's a new one. Listen, Ben, don't have anything to do with that man. He's evil.'

'No he's not, he's ... '

'I tell you, Ben. He's not just a small-time drug dealer, he's part of a big gang. Me and Johnny got done over by him. He promised us all sorts and then when the police got involved, he disappeared and we got the blame. That's what he does. Finds lads with time on their hands and promises them all sorts.'

'What?'

Mike nodded. 'Blackwood's not his real name. And no one knows where he lives.'

'But I've been to his place.'

'To his house?'

'Well, no, not to his house, but to some land he owns.'

Mike smiled into the darkness. 'He told you that, did he?'

Ben didn't answer.

'He'll tell you a lot of things,' said Mike. 'It's all lies.'

Ben could feel the sweat trickling down the back of his neck.

'You're just trying to scare me.'

'You *should* be scared. Blackwood's bad news.

He's left us alone since my Uncle Lash spread the word about him.'

'What do you mean?'

Mike grinned. 'Did he tell you he didn't like gypsies?'

'Yeah.'

'And he told *us* he was part Romany! He just says what you want to hear.'

Mike let go of Ben and folded his arms. 'But it don't do to try and cheat us. He knows that now.'

Ben swallowed. 'But there must be someone on the site he still deals with.'

'Yeah. Looks like there is.'

Neither of the boys spoke for a minute, then Mike sniffed.

'You'd better go, Ben. Tell Blackwood no one at the site wants to do business with him.'

Mike stood away from the driver's door and Ben jumped in. His hands were trembling so much that he had to have several goes at stabbing the key into the ignition.

Mike leant into the window.

'Seriously, Ben. Do yourself a favour. Keep away from Blackwood.'

Five

Ben drove back and parked the car in the road behind the rec. He turned off the engine and slumped over the steering wheel.

He'd have to tell Blackwood he hadn't delivered the package. But what if Mike was right? What if Blackwood was more than a small-time drug pusher? What if he *was* part of some gang?

Ben thought about Blackwood's big expensive car, the fancy watch and the smart clothes.

Where did all his money come from?

Suddenly his phone rang. He jumped and dug in his pocket for it.

Blackwood. 'I hear you didn't deliver the package to my client at the site.'

Ben's heart beat faster. 'No, there was no one there. I waited.'

There was a long silence, then, 'No one?'

'No,' said Ben.

'That's not what I heard.'

Ben dragged his hand through his hair. 'What do you mean?'

'My client rang just now. Said he was a few minutes late but then he saw you talking to someone else.'

'Yeah ... well, just a gypsy boy from school giving me a bad time.'

'So why did you lie to me, Ben?'

'I didn't. I just said the guy didn't show.'

'You said there was no one there.'

'Yeah, but I didn't mean ... '

Blackwood's voice cut him off. 'Never lie to me again, Ben, do you understand?'

'Yeah.'

'And get back down there right away. The guy's waiting for his delivery.'

'But I ... '

'Just do it!' said Blackwood and switched off his phone.

Ben was too scared to disobey. He started up the car and drove slowly back to the site. As he approached, he could see the figure of a man standing by the lane, smoking. The end of his cigarette was glowing in the dark.

Nervously, Ben got out of the car, holding out the package. The man came towards him. He took the package and turned to go.

'What about the money?'

The man laughed. 'You gonna make me pay, are you son?'

'You've got the goods,' said Ben, his voice sounding squeaky.

The man gave him a push. 'Wanna fight me for it?'

Ben shook his head.

'Tell yer boss he'll have to send someone bigger next time if he wants his money.' Then he spat on the ground before walking away.

Ben stood there for a few moments, his hands hanging by his side. What could he do? He didn't dare follow the bloke, but he was really scared of what Blackwood would say. Would he make him try and get the money?

Ben hadn't even reached the rec when his phone rang.

'You delivered the goods?' asked Blackwood.

'Yeah, but … '

'But what?'

'The bloke went off without paying.'

'WHAT?!'

'I'm sorry.'

'You're SORRY? That's not good enough. I told you, you *always* have to get the money first.'

There was silence. Then Blackwood spoke again.

'You realize you've cost me?'

Ben swallowed. 'Yes.'

'Well you'll have to make it up, Ben, and I know just how you can do that.'

Ben felt a twist of fear in his gut. What was he going to ask him to do?

'Meet me tomorrow, usual time. I'll tell you where later.'

Ben couldn't sleep that night. What would Blackwood ask him to do? He'd already done deliveries for him, and he'd been driving without a licence.

He was scared. He kept thinking of what Mike had said to him: 'Keep away from Blackwood.'

He knew it was wrong, but how could he stop? He enjoyed the smokes – they made him forget he hadn't got a future as a footballer – and he liked the money.

How else could he earn any money?

The next morning he lay in bed hearing Kate and Tess talking, getting breakfast, doing the usual things. It was all so normal.

'Ben!' Kate's voice drifted up the stairs.

He didn't answer.

'Ben!' Her voice was louder, crosser.

He grunted a response. Then she was opening the door into his room.

'Come on Ben, get up.'

'What for?'

Kate sighed. 'You can't lie in bed all day, Ben.'

'Why not? I'm tired.' He turned his face towards the wall.

Kate stood at the door.

'Go away, Mum,' muttered Ben.

'No I won't go away. We need to talk.'

' "We need to talk, we need to talk." Someone change the record.'

'We'll talk this evening,' said Kate firmly.

'I'm out.'

'Then I'll wait up until you get in.'

Ben sat up in bed, his hair tousled. 'What is it

you want, Mum? I'm learning a trade and I'm getting paid for it.'

'I want to meet this guy who's giving you work,' said Kate. 'I've spoken to Dad and we both agree. We need to know more about him.'

That's never going to happen.

Kate went downstairs and after a while Ben heard the front door slam.

He pulled the duvet over his head. What a mess. His whole life was a mess.

Later, he got up and made himself a cup of tea. He felt sick. He couldn't face anything to eat. As he was sitting at the kitchen table, staring out the window, his phone rang.

He dragged it out of his pocket. It was a number he didn't recognize.

'Yes?'

'Ben. It's Mike.'

Ben sat up and frowned. 'Mike!' Then, 'How did you get my number?'

'Never mind. Listen. About what I said last night. About Blackwood.'

'What about him?'

'D'you want to keep working for him?'

'I dunno,' said Ben. Then he said quietly, 'but I can't stop now, can I?'

'You smoking the funny fags?'

'Yeah.'

'Got you hooked, has he? And got you driving that car with no licence?'

Ben didn't answer.

'Look, it's how he works. 'Gets youngsters in too deep. Gives them little jobs and pays them, then he gets them on to the bigger stuff.'

'What do you mean?'

'You'll find out.'

Ben thought of what Blackwood had said to him last night.

You'll have to make it up, Ben, and I know just how you can do that.

'I don't know what to do.'

He couldn't believe he'd said that to the gypsy boy!

There was a long silence and Ben wondered whether Mike was still on the phone.

'Mike?'

'Yeah. I'm thinking. Look, we might be able to help you?'

The gypsies, help *him*!

'How?' said Ben. 'How could you help me?'

Mike laughed, hearing the suspicion in Ben's voice.

'Don't trust us gypsies, do you?'

'I … I didn't say that.'

'I know what you think of us, Ben. You've told us often enough. But I tell you summat. Blackwood's not scared of much, but he's scared of us. When me Uncle Lash got the word out about him, he was well scared.'

'What did your uncle say?'

Mike laughed. 'I dunno. I wasn't there, was I? But I guess he made sure word got back to Blackwood that it don't do to rile the gypsy men. And if you mess with their family they never forgive you.'

'But Blackwood's still dealing with someone on the site.'

'Yeah. I bin thinking about that. I guess whoever it was knew he'd be safe.'

'What do you mean?'

'Well, Blackwood's not gonna come to the site demanding money, is he? Not after what he did to me and Johnny. The men would laugh in his face.'

Ben couldn't believe that anyone would dare laugh at Blackwood.

'Blackwood was furious with me,' he said.

'I'll bet. Did he say you'd have to make it up?'

'Yeah.'

'That's how he works. He'll get you on to sommat bigger now.'

Ben's mouth was dry. What did it mean, 'something bigger'?

'What shall I do?'

There was a long silence. Then Mike said, 'Tell you what, Ben. Find out what he wants you to do. Then phone me.'

'You won't say anything to Tess?'

'No.'

Could he trust him?

'So, you gonna do that?' Mike asked.

'OK.'

What choice did he have?

'I'm not doing this for you, Ben. We'll be doing it 'cos we all hate Blackwood – or whatever his name is.'

'Thanks, Mike.'

Mike laughed. 'Taking help from a gypsy boy, eh?'

Ben didn't answer. He couldn't believe it himself.

Six

When Ben met up with Blackwood that evening, he was really scared. He was feeling so nervous that his hands were shaking. He was sure Blackwood would pick up on his fear.

But Blackwood didn't seem that angry. In fact, he seemed in a good mood. He put his arm round Ben's shoulders and Ben resisted the temptation to wriggle out of his grip.

'Never mind, son,' said Blackwood. 'So, we lost out to that gypsy scumbag. And you've learned your lesson.'

Ben nodded, not trusting himself to speak.

Blackwood released him and punched him lightly on the arm. 'I've got another job for you, Ben.'

'OK,' said Ben. His palms were sweating.

'Come for a drive with me,' said Blackwood. 'I don't like hanging around here. I'll explain in the car.'

Reluctantly, Ben climbed into the big car. He felt trapped as Blackwood drove off.

Ben's heart was racing. He checked his watch. They'd been gone a long time and they were miles from home.

'Where are we going?' he asked.

Blackwood patted him on the knee. 'You'll see. It's not far now.'

At last they pulled up. Ben didn't know where they were, but it was on the outskirts of a town, in a posh area. The street was lined with trees and there were big houses each side of the road.

'What are we doing here?' asked Ben.

Blackwood didn't answer immediately. He wound down the window and lit up a spliff. Then he handed one to Ben.

Ben took a drag and began to feel a bit calmer. What had Mike called them? Funny fags.

Blackwood pointed to a house a bit further down the street.

'Holiday time, isn't it?'

'What?'

'Big empty houses full of goodies,' said Blackwood.

Ben took another deep drag.

Is he saying what I think he's saying?

'Now,' continued Blackwood, still pointing at the same house. 'That's the only house on the street without an alarm, Ben.'

Ben nodded.

'And the people only left yesterday, so they'll be away for a couple of weeks.'

Ben turned to look at Blackwood, his eyes wide.

'You're not asking me to do a *robbery*?'

'Oh no, Ben, not on your own. You're not experienced enough. Not yet. No, I just want your help.'

Ben thought of Mum and Dad and Tess. He couldn't do this.

'I can't,' he began.

'Can't?' said Blackwood evenly. 'Oh yes, Ben. I think you can.'

Ben looked frantically about him. He noticed the name of the street, but it meant nothing to him. He tried the car door but it was locked. Even if he got away from Blackwood, he had no idea where he was. He'd be completely lost.

Blackwood leaned back in his seat. 'Of course, there's a bit of extra money in this job, Ben. It's a bit more complicated than just delivering packages.'

Ben's eyes were frantic. The spliff hadn't, after all, worked its magic this time. He just felt scared and alone.

'But it's a *crime!*' His voice came out as a squeak.

Blackwood laughed. 'A crime, Ben? And drug dealing and driving without a licence. What's that, eh?'

'Yeah, I know, but it's not … '

'Not what? Not so bad as stealing from people?'

Ben nodded miserably.

'A crime's a crime, Ben. Better get used to it. You're in too deep now.'

'I want to stop,' whispered Ben. 'I don't want to … '

Blackwood's voice was harsh. 'What you want doesn't matter, Ben. You're working for me and you'll do as I say. I can easily get someone to tell the police about you, you know. You can go to prison for drug dealing.'

'But then you'd ... '

'Don't be such a fool, boy. No one can ever trace it to me. I've made very sure of that.'

Ben stared at him. Blackwood went on. 'And what would your nice family say about that, eh? Your respectable mum and your bright little sister. And your dad. But he doesn't live with you, does he? No man about the place, is there?'

Ben swallowed. Was Blackwood threatening him? Saying that if Ben didn't do as he was told, he'd send someone round to do something bad to Mum or Tess?

Think.

Then he remembered Mike's words. 'Find out what he wants you to do, then phone me.'

He threw the rest of his spliff out of the window. He wasn't alone. Mike would help him.

'What do you want me to do?'

Blackwood patted his knee again. 'That's my boy,' he said, smiling.

And suddenly Blackwood was all nice again. 'I knew you'd see sense, Ben. You'll be an asset to the team.'

'Now,' he continued, shifting in his seat so he was looking directly at Ben. 'This is what I want you to do. You get out of the car and walk to that house. He handed Ben a phone. Sneak round the back and take some photos on this phone.

Ben nodded. 'What of? What shall I take photos of?'

'The back of the house. The garden. The side of the house.'

Ben looked puzzled. Blackwood smiled.

'I want you to case the joint for me Ben. So we can see the best way in.'

Slowly, Ben got out of the car, the phone in his hand. Blackwood started the engine and Ben looked back. 'Where are you going?'

'Don't panic. Just going to park up that side street, out of sight. Don't want any nosey neighbours spotting my car, do we? And Ben?'

'Yeah.'

'Don't draw attention to yourself.'

Ben pulled his hood over his head and walked slowly up the road, past several large houses until he came to the one that Blackwood had pointed out. Quickly he slipped in at the front gate and walked up the path, then round to the back of the house.

It was very quiet. The light was fading but Ben could see that the garden was beautiful. Flower beds full of colour and at the end of the garden some fruit trees. A high fence ran all round the garden, so it was completely private. It wasn't overlooked and no one would be able to see what was happening here.

Ben wondered who lived here. He took photos of the back door and all the windows, then he peered through some glass doors into a conservatory full of more plants. He'd never seen anything like it. These people must be really loaded.

He went back round the side of the house. There was another window there and, by standing on tiptoe, he managed to see in. A beautiful lounge with chairs and sofas and a massive telly and sound system.

Just as he was about to leave, he spotted some photos on a table inside the room, beneath the window. He saw a photo of a man and a woman and two children, all laughing, standing on top of a hill with their arms around each other. A real family. All together.

He didn't stay long and soon he was walking quickly back to the gate and along the road. He went down the side street to where Blackwood had parked his car.

And just as he was about to get in, he noticed that the number plate was different.

He said nothing to Blackwood, but showed him the photos he'd taken. Blackwood scrolled through them and grinned. 'Good stuff,' he muttered. 'It'll be a pleasure to relieve them of it.'

Ben swallowed. 'When are we going to do the job?' he asked.

Blackwood looked up sharply. 'You're keen all of a sudden,' he said. Then he went on, 'This job won't involve you, Ben. You've done your bit by taking the photos. But there's another one coming up where we'll need a nimble lad like you.'

Ben didn't dare ask for any more details.

Seven

It was late by the time Ben got home that evening, but Kate was still up. She was sitting in the kitchen in her dressing gown.

'Mum, why aren't you in bed?'

'I said we needed to talk, Ben.'

Ben slumped down in a chair beside her. He noticed how tired and worried she looked and suddenly he was really frightened. What if Blackwood carried out his threat? What if he sent some thug to hurt Mum or Tess?

Perhaps I can tell her what's been happening and she'll go to the police. But he couldn't, could he? Blackwood was too clever. No one would be able to pin anything on him. Ben would be the only one in trouble.

'I'm pleased if you're learning about cars, Ben,' said Kate.

'What? Oh. Yeah.'

'Tell me about the place you're working in.'

Ben looked up. 'Err. I work all over the place,' he said. 'I go and fix things for people.'

Kate frowned. 'And this man who's giving you work, John Davis was it? How did you meet him?'

Ben had forgotten he'd given Mum a false name.

'Er, through someone's dad.'

'Who?'

'No one you know.'

Mum frowned. 'I'd like to meet him.'

Ben looked up, but he couldn't meet her eyes. 'Yeah. Well, I'll try and fix it up,' he said.

Blackwood's never, ever gonna see her. Not if I can help it.

'Thanks, love,' she said. 'I'd feel happier if I knew more about him.'

She yawned and got up, scraping back her chair. 'I'm off to bed now.'

Ben watched her go, then he leant forward,

burying his head in his hands. Every time he lied to her he felt really bad. He glanced up at the clock. Was it too late to ring Mike? But he must speak to someone.

Mike's phone was about to go to voicemail, when he picked it up, his voice sleepy.

'Ben?'

'Mike. Did I wake you?'

'Doesn't matter. What happened?'

It was a relief to talk to someone who knew about Blackwood.

'He drove me miles, to these really posh houses.'

'Sounds like what he did with us,' said Mike. 'Did he make you go and case the joint, take photos and that?'

'Yeah.'

There was silence for a while, then Mike said. 'Watch it, Ben. Get out while you can. He's bad news.'

'I want to,' said Ben. 'But I'm scared.'

'He threaten you, did he?'

'Yeah. Talked about Dad not being around. About Mum and Tess.'

'You think he might do something to them if you don't do what he says?'

'Yeah.'

There was a long silence, and Ben wondered if Mike had gone back to sleep.

'Mike?'

'Yeah. I'm thinking.' Then he went on, 'Look, come round tomorrow morning.'

Ben swallowed. 'To the site?'

'You got a problem with that?'

'No.'

I have, though. I don't want to go round there.

'I'll see you tomorrow, then.'

'OK.'

'Oh, and Ben.'

'Yeah?'

'Don't come in that car of his. Get on yer bike.'

Ben bit back an angry reply. Of course he wouldn't be so stupid to drive it around the village in daylight. But he didn't say anything.

That night Ben slept badly and dreamt of being chased by Blackwood and the gypsies.

He was up early and made Kate some tea. She looked surprised.

'Thanks love,' she said and gave his arm a squeeze.

Ben couldn't look at her.

After breakfast he got his bike out of the shed. He hadn't used it in a while and it was dusty and covered in cobwebs. He found a pump and put air into the tyres.

Tess came out of the house and saw him. 'You off somewhere?'

He nodded, not trusting himself to speak. Suddenly he saw her as his little sister, not the annoying clever one who always seemed to get what she wanted. He saw her through Blackwood's eyes. Young and innocent. If Blackwood or his thugs touched a hair on her head … He closed his eyes. He had to protect her. Her and Mum, too. Even if it meant getting the gypsies involved.

'Have a good day, Tess,' he muttered.

Tess turned, surprised. She smiled at him. 'Thanks.'

'You off to the stables?'

'Yep. As if you care.'

'How's it going with that pony?'

She frowned. 'Fine. It's going fine.'

'Maybe I'll come and watch sometime?'

Tess stood there, her mouth open in surprise. 'OK,' she said slowly. 'If you want.'

Ben wiped off the worst of the dust from the bike's saddle and hopped on. It felt too small for him; he must have grown. He tested it out up and down the road for a while, until he was sure that Tess was out of sight, and then set off for the site.

As he rode under the motorway bridge towards the entrance to the site, Ben became more and more nervous. What if Mike wasn't there? What if he saw some of the other gypsy boys, boys he'd bad-mouthed at school?

He got off his bike and wheeled it between the vans. Several dogs barked at him, but there didn't seem to be anyone around. Then he saw a woman shaking a rug outside her van while she was carrying on a conversation with someone out of sight.

'Excuse me,' said Ben.

'Hello, love,' said the woman.

Ben cleared his throat. 'Er. I'm looking for Mike?'

'Mike? Oh he'll be down with the horses.'

She pointed back the way he'd come. 'Down that lane,' she said.

Ben pushed his bike down the lane, the hedges either side tall and in full summer growth. He came round a corner and saw a barred gate into a field. He stood there for a moment, watching nervously. There were several men at the far side of the field and he could see that Mike was with them. At first they didn't notice him and Ben watched as they groomed the ponies, black-and-white and brown-and-white cobs, and chatted and laughed. Then someone pointed to him.

Mike said something to the others, then he walked over to the gate, leading a pony behind him.

'Hi,' said Ben.

'Hi,' said Mike, and he went on grooming the pony.

Ben felt awkward. 'About what you said.'

'About Blackwood?'

'Yeah.'

'I bin thinking,' said Mike. 'I talked to some of the men about him.' Mike took a metal comb out of his pocket and started to get the knots out of the pony's mane.

'We're going to a horse fair tomorrow,' he said. 'Have to get all the horses looking good.'

Ben nodded. He knew nothing about horses. He waited for Mike to go on.

'This Blackwood fellow. He's a tricky one.'

'Tell me about it,' said Ben.

'Blackwood's not his real name. No one knows his real name. He changes it all the time. He called himself sommat else when he conned me and Johnny.'

Changes his name like he changes his number plates.

'So, he'd be hard to catch.'

Ben nodded.

Mike stopped grooming the pony for a moment and looked at Ben.

'Thing is. He never does the dirty work. He gets others to do that.'

'Like me,' said Ben, grimly.

'And me and Johnny, too,' said Mike. 'But he's never around when a job's being done. No one knows where he lives, so he's never bin caught.'

'So, even if I went to the police … '

Mike grinned. 'Don't go doing that, Ben. That's not going to do no good.'

'Then what?'

The pony blew through its nostrils and stamped its hoof. Mike stroked it.

'Blackwood – or whatever his name is – he ain't scared of much. But he's scared of the gypsy men. He knows me Uncle Lash has spread the word about him, so I doubt he'll try it on with gypsy boys again.'

'Yes, you said.'

'But even if the gypsy men found him and roughed him up,' said Mike. 'That won't stop him. He'll just move out of the area for a bit. He's got contacts all over.'

'How do you know?'

Mike fiddled with the pony's mane. 'I had a bit of trouble with a bloke up North,' he said. 'He knew Blackwood an' all.'

Ben frowned. 'But if he's not going to bother gypsies again … '

'Then why do we want to help you?' finished Mike. 'Like I said, we want him caught and locked up. He's caused us all kinds of grief. And I'll tell you sommat else, Ben. No one here could care less about you, after all the abuse you've given me, but I told them Blackwood might come after Tess if you didn't do what he wanted.'

He pointed over to the group of men on the other side of the field. 'They think the world of Tess.'

Ben looked down at the ground. 'So, have they got a plan?' he mumbled.

Mike nodded. 'Yeah. It could work an' all, but it depends on you, Ben.'

Ben licked his dry lips. 'What do you mean?'

'You'd have to keep your nerve.'

Eight

Mike and Ben walked back up to the site. A big old-fashioned wagon was standing at the entrance now. It hadn't been there earlier. Ben stared at it.

'What's that?'

Mike grinned. 'It's a vardo,' he said. 'That's what gypsies used to travel in, in the old days. My nan and granddad had one like this. We're taking it to the horse fair tomorrow.

Ben stared at the beautifully decorated wagon, with its cloth covering and bright colours.

'Want to look inside?' asked Mike.

Ben nodded and followed Mike up the steps. Mike showed him how everything worked; the sliding panels, the places for sleeping, the storage and the old-fashioned stove with its chimney going up through the roof.

'Where did the family sleep?'

'Parents and babies inside and the rest underneath.'

'Underneath?'

'Yep,' said Mike. He led Ben down the steps again and pointed under the wagon. 'They'd put a waterproof sheet, then hay, then another covering and the kids slept there.'

'You don't still ... ?'

Mike laughed. 'No. Not now. I got me own place that Dad built for me on the plot and there's a day room and we got a kitchen and shower and all. Come on, I'll show yer.'

When they walked into the day room, Lizzie was there, busy working on her jewellery, but she jumped up in surprise when she saw Ben.

'You're Tess's brother, ain't you?' She frowned and started to gather up her bits and pieces.

'Yeah,' said Ben. He could imagine what Tess had said about him.

'No need to move,' said Mike. 'I was just showing Ben how the dirty gypsies live.'

Ben blushed. 'Mike … '

'Come on,' said Mike. 'The men will be back now.'

Ben felt very nervous when he saw the group of men who had gathered near the old vardo. No wonder Blackwood was scared of them. They looked at him but didn't smile.

Then one of the men came up to him. 'Mike says you're Tess's brother.'

Ben nodded.

'She's a good lass.'

He nodded again, wondering where this was leading.

'And that you've had bother with this guy.'

'Yeah. Blackwood.'

Then suddenly the man grinned, the smile showing his white teeth in his tanned face.

'Blackwood! That's a new one. And you're going to help us get rid of him.'

Get rid of him. What does that mean?

When Ben didn't answer, the same man laughed, a full-throated laugh, and some of the others joined in.

'Don't look so scared, son. You'll be doing us all a big favour.'

Then they told Ben their plan.

A long time later, Ben wheeled his bike into the shed at home. He was still thinking about what he'd agreed to do. He was terrified, but if it worked ...

'Ben?'

He looked up. Tess was coming up the path. She frowned at him.

'Ben,' she said. 'You've been at the site, haven't you?'

'What?'

'You heard.'

'I ... '

'Lizzie just called. She told me she saw you there, with Mike. What's going on?'

Ben bit his lip. He'd have to level with her.

'I'm in trouble.'

She leant her bike up against the shed. 'It doesn't take a genius to work that out,' she said. 'What's happened?'

'Swear you won't tell Mum?'

'Is it that bad?'

Ben nodded.

'OK,' she said slowly. 'I swear.' She sat down on the grass and he crouched down beside her.

He told her everything. About Blackwood, the jobs he'd done for him and what he was being asked to do now.

She frowned. 'Oh Ben, you're such an idiot.' But she said it gently.

He didn't shout back at her but nodded silently. 'I know that now. But it was easy money, Tess.'

'So, where does Mike come in?'

'There was some bloke at the site. I had to make a delivery to him and Mike saw me. He guessed what had happened. He and Johnny had trouble with this guy before.'

'And he's going to help you?'

'Yeah. I hope so. He and some of the men.'

'What? They're going to do something to this Blackwood guy?'

Ben nodded. 'I can't tell you about it.'

'Don't do anything stupid, Ben. You might make things worse.'

'At least there's someone on my side,' he said. He got up and stretched. 'But it's only 'cos they all hate Blackwood and want to get back at him. And,' he added, 'they don't want to see you in any trouble.'

'What do you mean?'

'They don't care about me. But they all like you, Tess.'

He wasn't going to tell her about Blackwood's threats.

Tess stood up too. 'If Mike's decided to help, he won't let you down. He'll stick by you, even though you've given him so much grief.'

They walked up the path to the back door. Just as they were going inside, Ben whispered, 'Don't say anything to Mum.'

Tess shook her head.

That night, when Ben met up with Blackwood, it wasn't at the rec, as usual. Blackwood had phoned and told Ben to drive to an address some way away. Ben keyed it into the sat nav and set off.

He didn't enjoy driving the car any longer. He suspected it was stolen; if he was ever picked up he'd have a lot of explaining to do, and Blackwood – or whatever his real name was – would be nowhere around. The thrill he'd felt at first had all drained away and he was left just feeling very scared.

Blackwood was standing outside his car, smoking. He tossed his cigarette away when Ben drove up and parked behind him.

'What took you so long?'

Ben didn't answer. He'd driven as fast as he'd dared.

Blackwood was in a bad mood. He opened his car door and brought something out. 'Here,' he said, handing Ben a set of number plates and a torch. 'Put these on your car.'

Ben didn't ask questions. He knelt down in the road, removed the number plates and then screwed on the new ones, but he was fumbling with the screw driver, his nerves making him clumsy.

'Hurry up,' said Blackwood. 'We haven't got all night.'

Ben was trying to remember what the men at the site had told him to do. Ask questions, find out as much as you can. When he's going to do the robbery. What day, what time.

A car door slammed and another man got out of Blackwood's car. Ben noticed that he had a limp.

Ben's hands shook as he gave the old number plates back to Blackwood.

'I don't want them in my car,' said Blackwood. 'Put them in the back of yours.'

Blackwood jerked his head towards the other man. 'This is my mate. He's going to show you what to do.'

'Let's have the keys, son,' said the man, stretching out his hand. Wordlessly, Ben handed over the car keys and the man got into the driving seat.

'Get in, Ben,' said Blackwood. 'I'll see you later.'

Ben's heart was racing as the stranger drove him away. He looked across at him. He was small and wiry, with a shaved head. 'What's your name?' he asked.

The man gave a laugh. 'You can call me Bob,' he said. 'Not that it's any of your business.'

'Where are we going?'

'Nosey little sod, ain't you? You'll see when we get there.'

After that they drove in silence. This wasn't working out the way Ben had hoped, the way he'd talked it through with Mike and the gypsy men. And he couldn't get help from them now. They were all away at the horse fair for the weekend.

They drove down the main street of a town and Bob parked the car.

'See that shop over on the other side of the road?' he said, pointing to a large department store.

Ben nodded silently.

The man rubbed his hands together. 'They take

a lot of cash over the weekend,' he said. 'And they don't bank it until the Monday.'

Ask questions.

'How do you know?'

Bob put his finger to the side of his nose. 'I got my sources,' he said.

'What do you want me to do?'

'I'm not as nifty as I was, Ben,' said Bob. 'I got this gammy leg now. I want you to scout out the back for me.'

He handed Ben a phone.

'Is this Blackwood's phone?' asked Ben.

'Who?'

'The guy we just left. The guy with the Merc.'

'Told you his name was Blackwood, did he?' Again, Bob laughed. An irritating, high-pitched laugh.

'What's his real name, then?'

'Who knows? Anyway it's none of your business. And yeah, it is his phone. Now you stop talking and listen.'

Then Bob told him what he wanted. Photos of all the windows and doors at the back, and a close-up of the alarm.

'And cameras, too. They might have cameras. Spot where they are and keep out of range. You'll have to climb over that wall to get in,' said Bob. 'D'you reckon you can do that?'

Ben nodded. He couldn't wait to get away from Bob.

'Got everything, then?'

'Yeah.'

Ben ran down the side of the building, keeping in the dark shadows. Blackwood had told him to dress in dark clothes so he'd be hard to spot.

He'd have to take some photos with the phone, but he had to do something else as well.

Would he have time to do what the gypsy men had suggested?

He moved as quickly as he could, keeping his body flat as he dragged himself up and over the wall. He jumped to the ground and crept forward. He couldn't see any cameras, but he could see the alarm on the back of the building, winking red and green. He got as close as he could and took a shot of it, zooming in so that its make was clear.

Then he sat down, his back to the building, and got out his torch. As quickly as he could, he downloaded an app onto his phone as well as all the details of Blackwood's phone. He used his mum's card number to pay for the app.

'Sorry, Mum,' he muttered.

The app took ages to download and he sat there, sweating, thinking that Bob would come looking for him at any moment.

At least he won't be able to climb the wall with that gammy leg.

At last the download was complete. He took a whole lot more photos with Blackwood's phone, and a few with his own, before scrambling over the wall again and, keeping low and bent over, running back to the waiting car.

'What the hell took you so long?' Bob was pacing up and down beside the car.

'Sorry. I wanted to check everything out properly.'

Bob grunted and Ben handed back Blackwood's phone.

Nine

When they got back to Blackwood, he questioned them both.

'Ben, did you see any cameras?'

'No.'

'And you took photos of everything? Every corner?'

'Yeah. It's all on the phone.'

'Can Bob get over that wall if you help him?'

'Not without a ladder or something.'

'Then we'll need you to help him.'

Blackwood scribbled something down. Then he looked at the photos on his phone.

'Good,' he said. Then he showed them to Bob.

'Can you disable the alarm, Bob?'

'Yeah. No problem.'

'And you know about the safe?'

'Yeah, I got the combination from me source. It'll be dead easy.'

Bob tossed the keys of the other car to Ben and got into the passenger seat of the Merc. Blackwood stubbed out another cigarette and started getting into the driving seat.

Ask about times and places.

'When are we going to do the job?' asked Ben.

Blackwood hesitated. 'You'll find out,' he said. Then, just before he started the ignition, he wound down the window.

'How's that little gypsy-loving sister of yours?'

Both men laughed. Ben didn't answer, but he felt as though someone had punched him in the gut.

Ben waited until the Merc had driven away and then he phoned Mike. It was a long time before he picked up, and Ben was about to leave a message when there was a breathless reply.

'Ben. What's happening?'

Ben could hear a lot of noise in the background. Shouting and laughing. Sounds of the horse fair, he supposed.

'I've just left Blackwood. He's planning a safe-breaking job.'

Mike whistled down the phone. 'Hey that's serious stuff.'

Ben explained what had happened. And he told Mike about the tracking device he'd fitted.

'Great. And he didn't suspect you?'

Ben hesitated. 'I don't think so.'

How's that gypsy-loving sister of yours? Was that a general threat so he didn't grass on Blackwood? Or did he suspect something?

'No,' he said, more firmly. 'No, I'm sure he didn't.'

'So, when's he going to do the job?'

'He wouldn't tell me.'

'He's a slippery bastard.'

'But,' Ben went on. 'I think I know.'

'Yeah?'

'He's got this safe-breaking mate and he let something slip. He told me the place we sussed out, the department store. He said they don't take their money to the bank until Monday.'

'So it could be Sunday, then?'

'Yeah. Could be.'

'And it's Saturday night now.'

'And you're all at the horse fair!'

There was a burst of laughter in the background.

'Sounds like you're having a good time.'

'Yeah. It's great. Ask Tess.'

Ben didn't react. Only a few days ago, he'd still been so angry about Tess's friendship with the gypsies. Now he was beginning to understand.

'I gotta go now, Ben, but I'll phone in a bit. I'll talk to the men.'

'OK. And Mike?'

'Yeah.'

'Thanks, mate.'

'Huh! *Mate* is it now?'

Ben drove slowly home. When he parked the car in the usual place, he took the number plates from the back. He'd noted the new plates on the Merc, too. So he had a record of all the numbers. They could be useful.

He walked back home, and his head was so full of what had been happening that at first he didn't realize that someone was calling his name.

'Ben!'

He jumped and looked out into the darkness.

'Ben!' He recognized the voice this time and stood still, waiting. It was one of his friends from school who lived just down the road. He had a dog with him.

He came closer. 'Hi. I was just giving the dog a run before bed'

The dog ran up to Ben and he stroked its back.

'You OK, Ben?' said his friend.

'Me? Yeah.'

'Dreading next week?'

'What?'

'Results.'

Ben had completely forgotten that exam results came out next week.

'I know I've failed.'

'Come on, you don't ... '

'Yeah, I do. I didn't do any work.'

'What about the footie trials?'

'Didn't make the squad.'

'There's always the Tech. You could go to the Tech. Though there's some gypsies at the Tech, aren't there? You wouldn't like that!'

Suddenly Ben's anger flared. 'Nothing wrong with gypsies,' he said and started to walk off.

His friend laughed. 'I can't believe you just said that. Not after all the grief you've given them.'

Ben didn't answer.

The lights were on in the house when Ben got back. Kate and Tess were sitting in the kitchen, chatting. They looked up when he came into the room and Ben suddenly felt protective. How could he do this to them? How could he put them in danger?

He'd been such an idiot, getting involved with Blackwood.

Tess met his eye and he knew she'd want to know what had happened, but she said nothing.

She's a pain, my little sister, but she won't grass on me.

Kate stood up and went to put the kettle on. 'Want a cuppa, Ben?' she asked.

'Yeah. Thanks.' He sat down at the table.

'We've been talking about the show,' said Tess, filling the silence of unasked questions.

Ben frowned. 'The show?' He had no idea what she was talking about.

'The show at the riding stables. You know. I'm competing on Flame.'

Ben tried to concentrate. 'Oh yeah. When's that?'

'Next weekend. Last weekend of the holidays.

Dad's coming down and he's bringing Emma and Tom.'

Ben raised his eyebrows. Emma and baby Tom had never been to their house. Kate had her back to them, so they couldn't see the expression on her face, but she said nothing.

Tess mouthed 'It's OK. She's OK about it.'

'Right,' said Ben, aloud.

It was some sort of breakthrough if Mum was agreeing to seeing Dad with Emma and Tom down here. But he couldn't think about that now. All he could think about was Blackwood and what was going to happen next.

He gulped his tea and scraped back his chair. 'I'm off to bed. See ya.'

He was exhausted, but his sleep was full of dreams of Blackwood. His phone was by his bed, kept switched on all night, but there were no messages when he woke in the morning. For a moment he felt good, refreshed, but then the whole situation came back to him and he felt sick with worry. Mike had promised to phone him back and he'd not heard from him.

Perhaps all the men were too busy at the horse fair to care. Perhaps they weren't going to help, after all.

It was mid morning before he could get hold of Mike. There was still a lot of noise in the background and the line kept cracking up. Ben had difficulty hearing.

'Sorry. Reception's really bad,' said Mike. 'Did you get Blackwood's phone?'

'Yeah, I can track it from mine, OK. When will you be back?'

'Some time tonight. Not sure when.'

Some time tonight. That could be too late.

'I'll phone when we leave,' said Mike. And then the line went dead.

For the rest of the day, Ben couldn't settle to anything. Kate and Tess were both out, but he couldn't stay in the house. He went outside and found himself walking towards the gypsy site. It was a long way from where he lived, but it gave him a focus and, as he strode down the village street and towards the Tech, it cleared his head a bit.

At least Blackwood wouldn't come looking for him here. Blackwood would never show his face at the site again.

When he reached the site, he went down the lane to the field. There weren't many horses in it now, most of them were at the horse fair. Ben leant over the gate, tired from his long walk, scared about what would happen. He was so absorbed in his thoughts that he didn't hear the man approach until he was almost upon him.

'Well, if it's not the little messenger boy!'

Ben whipped round.

Oh God, no!

He recognized the man. It was the guy who had taken delivery of the package.

Ben tried to run, but the man held him fast.

'It's OK, lad. Don't look so scared. I'll not harm you.'

But he was blocking Ben's way out. Ben swallowed nervously as he watched the man take a tin from his pocket.

'Want a funny fag?'

Ben shook his head and watched as the man rolled himself a spliff. He lit it slowly, his eyes not leaving Ben's face.

The man took a long drag. 'You work for this Blackwood guy?'

Ben didn't know what to say. His shoulders sagged. He couldn't pretend any longer.

'I was stupid,' he muttered. 'I liked the money.'

The man grinned – and suddenly he didn't look so threatening.

'Yeah,' he said. 'He does that. He promises young lads the world.' He went on. 'He tried it with two of our boys.'

Ben nodded. 'Mike and Johnny. I know.'

The man laughed. 'It don't do to mess with family. We put the frighteners on him, spread the word about him.'

'I heard.'

They were silent for a while.

'Why did you buy stuff from him again, then?' asked Ben.

The man shrugged. 'I was skint and I needed some weed. I knew he wouldn't come down here himself. I knew he'd send some poor sucker. And I was right, wasn't I?' He laughed again and took another drag.

'I'm no angel myself,' he went on, 'but that Blackwood's bad. You want to keep away from him, son. He's a slippery devil an' all. No one knows where he lives. And he never does robberies himself. Never does the dirty work.'

Ben hesitated. Could he trust this guy? Maybe, if the others didn't get back in time, he'd help? He took a deep breath.

'I think he's doing a robbery tonight.'

'What!'

Ben nodded. 'Mike and some of the other men, they said they'd come. We're gonna try and trap him.'

The man sucked in his breath. 'That's risky, son. He's got you involved, has he?'

'Yeah. And if I say no … '

'I can guess. Threatened you, has he?'

'Yes. Says he'll come after my mum and Tess.'

'Little Tess, the gorger rider? She your sister?'

Ben nodded.

'She's a good lass.'

Ben nodded. He didn't feel the familiar pang of jealousy.

'So, what's the plan?'

Ben told him.

The man whistled. 'That's clever, that is. Track him to where he lives. Tell you what, son, I'll come along too. I'd like to teach that bastard a lesson and all.

He took a phone from his pocket. 'Me name's Shorty. Here, I'll give you me phone number.'

Ten

Ben took his time walking back up to the village. As he passed the Tech, he stopped. He suddenly wanted to see Mum.

He went through the doors into the reception. There was a conference going on and people were busily walking around. Several greeted Ben, knowing that he was Kate's son.

'You'll find your mum in the office,' said one.

She was there at her desk, speaking to someone on the phone. She looked up as he came in the door and smiled, surprised. She finished the call and came round to the front of her desk and gave him a hug.

It almost finished him. If only she knew the trouble he was in.

'Hello love,' she said, releasing him. 'This is a nice surprise.'

'I was passing,' he said, realizing at once how mad this sounded. You'd only pass the college if you were on the way to the site.

He went on, quickly. 'Just wanted you to know that I charged something to your card.'

She frowned.

'It's OK, Mum. Just an app for my phone. I've got the money for it.' He dug in his pocket and drew out some of Blackwood's money.

Dirty money. He smiled to himself. At least he'd spent it on something which might trap the man.

He left the office before she had time to question him and he turned back at the door and waved.

'You going out again tonight?' she asked.

He nodded.

For the last time, hopefully. Hopefully he'd be shot of Blackwood.

But it could all go horribly wrong.

At six o'clock Ben was at the rec as usual, but there was no phone call from Blackwood, no phone call from Mike.

Ben felt very alone. He sat on the bench in the rec, his phone in his hands. He heard a clock strike seven in the distance.

It had never been this late before. Ben fiddled with his phone, trying out the tracking app. It worked! He could see where Blackwood was and he was a long way from the place he planned to rob.

But maybe that's what he did. Kept well away.

Or maybe Blackwood wasn't planning the robbery tonight. But then that man with the bad leg had said that the weekend money from the store didn't go to the bank until Monday.

Blackwood didn't know he'd let on. He'd be furious if he'd known.

When, finally, the phone rang, Ben jumped.

Blackwood's voice was harsh. 'Get in the car and come to where you met me last night,' he said.

'Will you be there?'

'Of course I'll be there. Now, get a move on.'

Ben phoned Mike, but he couldn't get through. Was Mike still at the horse fair, still in the mobile dead spot?

He'd try again in a few minutes. He had to contact him, let him know what was happening. He walked away from the rec, round the corner to to the place he kept the car. He stopped short. There was a group of people nearby.

What are they doing? There's never usually anyone here.

Ben looked at the group. Two women and a man, and they seemed in no hurry to leave. He recognized them and they greeted him as he walked past. He daren't get in the car. They would know his age. Know he wasn't old enough to drive.

He walked on, round the corner, and waited as the minutes ticked by.

Hurry up!

While he was waiting, he tried Mike again. But still no response. He scrolled down to the other number, Shorty's number. Could he trust the guy?

He didn't have a choice. Time was running out and he couldn't get hold of Mike. He pressed *Call* and waited, his hands sweating as he gripped the phone tightly.

Shorty answered immediately. 'You heard from the others yet, Ben?'

'No. I can't get through. Listen. Blackwood's

been in touch and I've got to drive to the same place. The place I told you about.'

'So it looks as though he's planning the job for tonight?'

'Seems that way.'

'OK, lad. Leave it with me. I'll keep trying the others for you, but if I can't get them I'll sort something out.'

Will he? I can't be sure.

At last the people by the car walked off and Ben was able to drive away. He was so nervous that he missed a couple of turns and had to go back. He knew that Blackwood would be angry.

'Where the hell have you been?' he said, when Ben finally turned up.

'Sorry. I got a bit lost.'

'Why d'you think I put a sat nav in that car?'

'Sorry.'

Blackwood grunted and Bob, the man with the limp, got out of the Merc. He brought a whole lot of tackle from the car and handed it to Ben.

'Put that in yer car,' he said, 'and give me the keys.'

Ben took the stuff and put it on the back seat. There were some tools, a collapsible ladder and a big canvas bag.

Blackwood got back in the Merc. 'See your later,' he said, and watched as Bob and Ben drove away.

When they got to the store, Bob parked close to the back entrance.

'We gonna do the job now?' asked Ben.

Bob grunted. 'Whatcha think?' said Bob, putting on a pair of thin gloves and flexing his fingers.

Suddenly, Ben's phone rang.

'Give that to me,' said Bob, making a dive for Ben's pocket, but Ben twisted away from him.

'Sorry, I'll switch it off.'

'Stupid little sod,' muttered Bob.

Ben just had time to see Mike's number come up before he switched off the phone.

''Give me that,' repeated Bob.

Don't let him take my phone.

'It's off now, Bob,' said Ben. 'It won't ring again. It was only my mum.'

Bob grinned. 'Yer mum, eh? Does she know where you are?'

'Course not. *As if.*'

'You keep it that way, boy. You don't want anything to happen to your mum, do you?'

Ben said nothing. Before Bob could ask for his phone again, he took the gear out of the back seat and started walking to the wall at the back of the store. Bob followed him, slowed up by his limp. They kept to the shadows.

Sunday night. The place was dead. No one around.

'Right son,' said Bob. 'Set up the ladder.'

The ladder was very light and Ben soon had it ready. Bob scrambled up it awkwardly. Ben followed, then heaved it over the other side so Bob could get down. Next, they set it up beneath the alarm and Ben watched as Bob took off the covering and carefully cut some wires. He worked silently, with a spot torch which could hardly be seen from below.

What am I doing? I'm deep in now. Accessory to robbery.

Ben held the ladder as Bob came down.

'Put that ladder back near the wall,' said Bob. 'And watch for anyone coming.' He handed the tools back to Ben. 'And hang onto these. I don't need them now.' He took something out of his pocket and knelt down by the back door.

Ben put the ladder back and then watched as Bob fiddled with the lock. He worked silently and soon there was a click and the door opened.

Ben started to follow Bob inside, but Bob put his hand on his chest.

'I don't need you inside,' he said. He pointed to the canvas bag. 'Hand me that bag. You wait here. Keep out of sight – and if anyone comes, you tell me. OK?'

'OK,' whispered Ben.

He watched Bob go inside the building, quiet as a cat, and close the door behind him.

Ben crept into a dark corner where the wall met the building and made himself as small as he could. He switched on his phone and punched Mike's number. He picked up.

'Hi. Where are you?'

'Mike. At last!' he whispered. 'We're doing the job, right now.' He could hear the tremor in his voice as he told Mike where the car was parked.

'Hang in there, Ben. You're doing great. Shorty filled us in. We're on our way. Just act natural. Phone when it's over.'

'The guy tried to take my phone.'

'Don't let him. And don't let Blackwood get it.'

'I'd better go.'

'We'll see you later.'

'I hope so.'

Ben's teeth were chattering even though the evening was warm. Time ticked by and he kept checking his watch.

Finally, he saw the back door open and Bob emerged. Ben could see that the canvas bag was heavy and he went over to help.

I should have worn gloves, too. They'll find my prints all over.

Bob was very pleased. 'Good haul,' he said, rubbing his hands together. 'OK, son, let's get outta here.'

It was harder, getting the heavy bag over the wall, but they managed it and soon had everything stowed in the car. Bob whistled tunelessly as he drove away.

'You're clever at locks and stuff,' said Ben, trying to sound as natural as possible.

Bob stopped whistling. 'Yeah. I done a few in my time.' He changed gear and swung the car round a corner. ''Course I could do a lot more before I did me leg.'

'How did that happen?'

'Work injury,' he said, and let out one of his cackling laughs.

They met up with Blackwood – in a different place this time.

He's a clever man. He moves about all the time. No wonder no one can catch up with him.

Blackwood was in a good mood when they

transferred everything to the Merc. He patted Ben on the back.

'Well done, son.'

He handed him some notes. Ben could hardly bear to take them.

'I'll be in touch,' said Blackwood, as Bob climbed in beside him. Ben raised his hand and watched them drive away.

As soon as they were out of sight, he phoned Mike.

'OK, they've gone. Where are you?'

Mike laughed. 'Just up the street.'

And then Ben heard an engine fire and saw a truck emerge from a side street. Mike and several of the men, including Shorty, piled out of the truck. Ben had never been so pleased to see anyone in his life.

'Let's have your phone, son,' said Shorty, grinning. 'This time, Blackwood's not getting away.'

'Do you want me to come with you?'

'No. Best leave it to the men. Take Mike back, too.'

Eleven

When Ben got back to the village and put the car in the usual place, he locked it up and chucked the keys in the bushes.

I'm never going near that car again.

Mike laughed. 'Don't worry, Ben. You'll be OK now.'

'How can you be so sure?'

'There's sommat I didn't tell you.'

Ben frowned. 'What's that?'

Mike rubbed his chin. 'I called the cops.'

'What!'

'Yeah. I know. But remember I told you about that gypsy cop who was good to me and Johnny when we got done over by Blackwood?'

Ben nodded into the darkness.

'Well. I got a fit of conscience. Felt bad about the guy. So I talked it over with the men and we decided to tell the cop that Blackwood was up to his old tricks again.'

'You told him about the robbery?'

'Yeah. They were watching.'

'What! And they didn't do anything?'

'They wanted to catch Blackwood with stuff in his car. So they're following him now, with your phone. That way, they'll know where he lives and they'll have evidence to put him away.'

'What about the men? I thought they wanted to put the frighteners on him.'

'Oh, they will. For once, the gypsies and the cops agree on sommat.'

'So they're all going to confront Blackwood.'

'Yep. And find out who he really is and where he really lives. Now that we've got that tracker, he can't get away.'

The police came to see Ben the next day and he told them everything. It was a relief to come clean, to them, to Mum. And they were really nice to him. They'd been after Blackwood for years and were grateful to Ben for helping catch him. He couldn't believe it; they let him off with a caution – and they even gave him his phone back.

It took a few days for Ben to hear all the details. He met Shorty down at the site.

'It was a good night's work, that,' he said.

'Where does he live?' asked Ben.

'Miles away. Next county. Thought we'd never get there, but it was worth it. He lives in a fancy house in a fancy street there. The police surrounded it minutes after he got in. Caught him red-handed.'

'What about you? Were you there, too?'

'Yep. Soon as the cops had done their stuff, we just strolled in to say hello. Let him know we knew where he lived, too. And his real name.'

'Bet he was surprised.'

'Surprised! He was gob-smacked. Serve the little creep right. He'll get banged up for a good long time now and he'll never try anything on in this part of the world again. And he'll not bother you again, son. Not now he knows you're friendly with us gypsies.'

Friendly with the gypsies. Well, he was, wasn't he?

Shorty slapped him on the back. 'Only one problem.'

'What's that?'

'I'll have to find another supplier.'

Ben looked at him.

'Don't look at me like that, Ben. Things 've bin bad for me. It helps me forget.'

The exam results came through a week later. Ben hadn't done quite as badly as he'd expected. He'd scraped a few passes. Kate didn't give him grief about it. She just said 'Not too bad, love,' and left it at that.

Ben was the one who decided.

'Mum,' he said one evening. 'I'll do retakes.'

Kate hugged him.

'Get off!' said Ben, but he was smiling.

He went on, 'Then maybe I'll go to the Tech, learn a trade.'

'That's a great idea, Ben.'

He hesitated, scuffing his trainer on the ground. 'I'm not clever, like Tess. I couldn't go to uni.'

'It wouldn't suit you love. I know that. But you *are* clever. You're brilliant at sport. And you love cars. Maybe a mechanic's course?'

Ben didn't want to think about cars. The police had towed away the car that Blackwood had let him drive.

'Maybe,' he said. 'There's plenty of time.'

'And you never know,' said Kate. 'You might get into the footie squad next time.'

Ben shrugged. He wouldn't pin his hopes on that. Not this time.

It was the last Saturday of the holidays, the day of the show at the riding stables. Tess had already left the house and Kate was yelling up the stairs to Ben.

'Come on love, we'll be late.'

Ben shuffled out of his bedroom, hopping on one leg as he put on his shoes.

'I can't believe I'm going to those poxy riding stables. It'll be full of stupid little girls on their stupid poncy ponies.'

Kate grinned. 'You know perfectly well it's not like that. And anyway, we're going to support Tess. It's a big day for her.'

'Yeah.' Ben pulled a T-shirt over his head and then ran a hand through his hair. 'When's Dad coming?' he asked.

For a moment, the smile left Kate's face. 'He's going straight to the stables,' she said.

'It'll be good to see little Tom again.'

'Yes,' said Kate slowly. 'It will. He's lovely.'

Neither of them mentioned Emma.

When they reached the riding stables, there were so many cars they had trouble parking. They could hear the riders being announced over the loudspeaker. Kate checked her watch. 'Tess isn't on yet,' she said. 'Her class isn't until later.'

'Huh!' said Ben. 'I could've had another hour in bed.'

He looked around him. There was a big yard full of stables and then a open area with a roof over it. Kate nudged him. 'That's called a ménage,' she said.

'What?'

'It's where they school the ponies, do indoor exercising.'

'Quite the expert, aren't you?'

Kate grinned. 'I've learnt a few things,' she said.

They walked on to join the crowds of people round the main show ring. There were judges sitting on chairs at one end and a whole lot of jumps set out in the show ring itself. Some were made of brushwood; there was a gate and several jumps which were made of poles. In the field behind the show ring there were lots of riders on their ponies, practising.

Kate grabbed Ben's arm. 'They all look so smart,' she said. 'I feel really nervous for Tess. D'you think she'll be OK?'

The next class was announced and a small girl trotted into the ring on her pony. A bell sounded and she put her pony at the first jump. She made a few mistakes and at the end of her round the announcer said, 'Eight faults'.

Kate looked at her watch. 'Dad should be here soon,' she said.

Ben was already bored. 'I'll go and look for him.'

He pushed his way through the crowds and walked round the grounds.

'Ben!'

He turned and saw Mike there. And not only Mike but his mum and dad and Lizzie and a couple of younger children, too. It was the first time he'd seen Mike's family all together.

A proper family. Not like ours.

He smiled at Lizzie, but she looked down at her feet.

'Tess is over there,' said Mike, pointing to the practice ring. She's in the next class.'

Tess was mounted on Flame, talking to Dad and Emma.

'Thanks,' said Ben. 'I'll go and wish her luck.'

By the time he reached the practice ring, Kate had spotted Tess and she'd gone over to join Dad, Emma and little Tom. They were an awkward group.

Dad greeted Ben with relief – and Tom ran up to him and hung onto his legs. Ben laughed and picked Tom up, swinging him round. The awkwardness evaporated and soon they were all chatting to Tess, wishing her luck, saying how good she looked, how good Flame looked. But Kate and Emma stood well away from each other.

Then Tess's class was announced. She looked round anxiously. 'Are Mike and Lizzie here?' she asked. 'They promised they'd come.'

Ben nodded. 'Yep. The whole family.'

Tess smiled. 'I've got to go. Wish me luck.'

They all walked away from the practice ring and found a good place to stand where they could see the competition. Tess's number was quite high, which meant lots of competitors would go in before her. Lots of the riders had faults, but there were several clear rounds, too.

Someone tapped Ben on the shoulder and he

turned round to see Mike and the rest of his family standing behind him. He grinned at them, but before he could say anything, Tess's name was announced and she came trotting into the ring on Flame.

Ben heard murmuring behind him and caught the words 'she's done a great job with that mare'.

Despite himself, Ben was nervous – and excited – for Tess.

'She looks amazing,' said Dad. Emma nodded and glanced across at Kate, whose eyes were fixed on Tess.

They all held their breath as Tess approached the first jump – and the next, and the next.

Then she came to the last one, sailed over it and cantered out of the ring, leaning forward and patting Flame's neck.

Both families let out a cheer.

'Clear round! That's fantastic,' said Emma and she looked over at Kate.

'She's done brilliantly.'

Kate nodded, her eyes bright with tears.

Ben turned to talk to Mike and his family. 'What happens now?' he asked.

'Jump off,' said Mike.

'What's that mean?'

'The riders with clear rounds jump again, against the clock.'

Soon they were all listening to Mike and his dad explaining what would happen next.

'They'll change the course,' said Mike. 'And make the jumps higher.'

Kate gasped. 'They look so big already.'

Mike grinned. 'She'll manage,' he said. 'She's a rare rider.'

There were six riders in the jump off. Tess would be the last to go. They watched the other riders. The first rider had twelve faults, the second had four faults, then the third had a clear round. Ben looked at the big clock on the side of the ring. He was getting the hang of this now. To win, Tess would have to get a clear round and be faster than the other riders with clear rounds.

The next rider had a clear round, too, but the one after that knocked down two jumps. 'Eight faults,' said the announcer.

Then it was Tess's turn.

Ben felt his whole body tense as she trotted in. She looked so confident, so at ease, and the pony's coat gleamed in the sunlight.

His little sister.

She approached the first jump. She was going

really fast and he held his breath as she got close. She knocked the top pole and it rattled in its cups but it didn't fall. And then she was on to the next. The gate. He noticed how she slowed the pony, getting its stride right before they jumped.

'Yeah!' Ben punched the air. 'Go Tess!'

He felt someone grab his arm and knew it was Mike, jumping every jump with Tess in his head, willing her on, just as he was.

There was the big spread coming up and again, Tess approached it fast, but Flame tucked up her legs and cleared it.

Only two more to go. But the clock was ticking.

The brush fence was more forgiving and they took that easily, then Tess took the short cut, meaning that she approached the last fence at an awkward angle.

'What's she doing? She'll never make it,' he gasped. But then he realised. She was taking a risk, but if she didn't slice a few seconds off her time, she would be slower than the other two clear rounds. She galloped towards the jump and the mare had to twist her body in mid air. Again the pole on top rattled, but it stayed put.

She let Flame have her head and they raced out of the ring.

A huge cheer went up. She'd done it! Her clear round was the fastest.

Ben's family and Mike's family cheered loudest of all. Ben thumped Mike on the back, and Lizzie and her mum were jumping up and down with excitement, as were the younger children. Emma hugged Kate and, to Ben's amazement, Kate returned her hug. They were both crying.

Dad put Tom on his shoulders and they watched as Tess came into the ring to receive her red rosette.

Ben turned to Mike, grinning. 'Not bad, eh?'

But it was Mike's dad who replied. 'Not bad for a gorger girl,' he said, and he was grinning fit to bust.

The Travellers

Four people, one story

Rosemary Hayes lives in Cambridgeshire with her husband and an assortment of animals. She worked for Cambridge University Press and then for some years she ran her own publishing company, Anglia Young Books. Rosemary has written over forty books for children in a variety of genres and for a variety of age groups, many of which have been shortlisted for awards.

Rosemary is also a reader for a well known authors' advisory service and she runs creative writing workshops for both children and adults.

To find out more about Rosemary, visit her website: **www.rosemaryhayes.co.uk**

Follow her on twitter: **@HayesRosemary**

Read her blog at **www.rosemaryhayes.co.uk/wpf**